Charlie Goes Camping

For my Mum and Dad X. – C.W.

For Toby "Toto" Ridgway. – T.W.

An Imprint of Sterling Publishing
387 Park Avenue South
New York, NY 10016

Text © 2011 by Carrie Weston
Illustrations © 2011 by Tim Warnes
Charlie Goes Camping was originally published in English in 2011
as *Bravo Boris*. This 2012 custom edition is published exclusively by
Sandy Creek in arrangement with Oxford University Press.

ISBN 978-1-4351-4082-0

For information about custom editions, special sales, and premium and corporate purchases, please contact
Sterling Special Sales at 800-805-5489 or specialsales@sterlingpublishing.com

Manufactured in China

Lot #:
2 4 6 8 10 9 7 5 3 1
11/11

Carrie Weston • Tim Warnes

Charlie Goes Camping

Sandy Creek
NEW YORK

The day that Miss Cluck took the class camping, everyone was very excited.

When Miss Cluck said that it was almost time to set off, all the animals squealed with delight.

Leticia the rabbit
carried her butterfly net.

Maxwell the mole
clutched his Teddy.

The little mice
each had a basket.

Fergus the fox cub
was given the map.

Leticia

Maxwell

And Charlie was put
in charge of . . .

absolutely everything else!
For Charlie was an enormous,
hairy, scary, grizzly bear . . .
but he was also rather kind and helpful.

"Bravo!"
said Miss Cluck
as Charlie heaved the
huge bag on his back.
"What would we
do without you?"

"Phew!"

Mini Beasts

Scrap

Miss Cluck and her class set off through the woods.

"Whee!"

Leticia chased after butterflies.

Fergus puzzled over the map.

Maxwell got Teddy stuck up a tree.

And the mice struggled with their baskets.

Eventually Charlie caught up with them all.

Poor Miss Cluck
blew her whistle.
"This really won't do,"
she said, "we must
stay together."

"But we're tired!"

Then Charlie had an idea.

He found room for everything in his bag. Even the tired mice.

"Bravo, Charlie!" cheered his friends.

Before long they came to a little bridge.

Charlie and Leticia dropped twigs into the stream.

"Come on, Charlie!"

"Go, Leticia!"

Then everyone rushed to the other side of the bridge to see whose would come out first.

But somehow,
Charlie forgot about
the bag on his back.

Somehow,
Maxwell's Teddy
went
splash!
into
the
water.

Somehow,
the mice managed
to cling on.

Maxwell let out an enormous wail.
"Oh, Charlie!" he cried.

Poor Charlie felt so clumsy and ashamed.

Miss Cluck carefully leaned over the bridge with Leticia's butterfly net, but it was no good. Teddy was floating away.

Charlie decided it was time to be very brave. He leapt into the water . . .

splash!

all the way
up to his
hairy knees!

Charlie scooped Teddy safely out of the water.
Now there were two dripping-wet bears.

And Maxwell
hugged
them both.

"Charlie is the biggest, bravest, best bear!" said Maxwell.

"Bravo, Charlie!"

"Bravo, Charlie!" agreed Miss Cluck. "Now let's set up camp before there are any more accidents."

The animals gathered around
while Miss Cluck explained
how to build a tepee.
It all sounded very easy.

Leticia and Maxwell collected long sticks.

The mice chewed off
some lengths of rope.

"Nibble!"   "Nibble!"

Charlie helped
Fergus spread
out the canvas.

Then they all tried to put it together.

But it was not easy . . . not at all easy.

Once the tepee was up, the fun really began. Miss Cluck got out a new box of chalk and let everyone draw on the tepee.

Camp Cluck

It looked wonderful.
Charlie put Maxwell's Teddy on top to dry . . .

and off they went
to pick berries for
dinner. Miss Cluck
showed them which
ones were good to eat.

Charlie carried the full baskets
while the other animals hurried
excitedly back to camp.

But they
were in
for a shock!

For their wonderful tepee wasn't
quite so wonderful any more.
Someone had drawn on Miss Cluck's face.
Someone had pulled down all the sticks . . .

and someone was going to be in **BIG** trouble!

Miss Cluck was very, very angry indeed. She marched straight up to the bulging canvas, reached underneath, and pulled out . . .

two very naughty little wolf cubs.
The cubs wriggled and struggled.

"Do your parents know you are out in the woods
alone?" asked Miss Cluck in her firmest voice.

"We don't care!" yelled one of the cubs rudely.
"Our daddy is a **big,**
bad
wolf!"

"He's much **bigger** than you," said the other,
even more rudely, "and he **eats chickens** for ..."

The naughty little wolf cubs turned on their heels and fled. Charlie was most confused.

"Aaaaagghhh!"

"**Oh, Charlie,** what a brave bear you are," smiled Miss Cluck, "now let's put the tepee back together."

"Bravo for hairy, scary Charlie!"

That evening Charlie and his friends ate a dinner of toasted marshmallows and berries until the sun went down.

Then Miss Cluck got out her guitar and they sang songs under the stars.

"Kum Bay Ya!"

"Mmm yummy!"

Charlie felt his eyelids grow heavy.
It was tiring being a big, brave bear.
"I think I might go to bed now," he yawned.

"Sleep tight!"

"Good night, Charlie."

"Night night!"

Charlie snuggled down
happily inside the tepee
and was soon snoring.

A little later, Fergus, then Leticia, Maxwell with Teddy, the mice, and Miss Cluck crept into the tepee.

There wasn't much room but nobody minded a bit. After all, everyone had a nice, soft place to sleep . . .

even Miss Cluck.
"Bravo, Charlie," she whispered
as she fell asleep.